The curious case of Benjamin Button

Choix des textes et notes

Lionel Hurtrez
Agrégé d'anglais

La collection « Histoires faciles à lire » s'adresse à tous ceux qui ont envie de lire des textes littéraires en version originale. Les ouvrages regroupent par thèmes les textes d'auteurs connus et reconnus dans chacune des langues proposées. Les textes sont présentés en version intégrale ou en version adaptée et simplifiée, selon le niveau de difficulté. L'essentiel du vocabulaire nécessaire est traduit sur la page de gauche pour une lecture facile et rapide.

Quatre niveaux pour quatre groupes de lecteurs :
Niveau 1 : super facile pour débutants et adolescents (A2 vers B1)
Niveau 2 : facile (B1)
Niveau 3 : intermédiaire (B1 vers B2)
Niveau 4 : avancé (B2 vers C1)

Édition et mise en pages : Tiffany Thomas
Couverture : Camille Maury
Image de couverture : iStock © duncan1890

5 avenue de la République, 75011 Paris
www.ophrys.fr

ISBN: 978-2-7080-1648-4

ISSN: 2551–2366

Dans la même collection aux éditions Ophrys :

en **espagnol** :

- *Anaconda, H. Quiroga*, 2018 (Niveau 1)
- *Horror, amor y humor*, R. Arlt, 2018 (Niveau 2)
- *Cuentos y relatos de pequeños y mayores*, G. Nájera, R. Delgado, J. Martí, 2019 (Niveau 3)
- *Cuentos de amor, de locura y de muerte*, H. Quiroga, 2020 (Niveau 2)
- *La cabeza del dragón*, R. del Valle Inclán, 2020 (Niveau 3)
- *Soñata de Otoño*, R. del Valle Inclán, 2021 (Niveau 3)
- *Historias morales y amorales*, J. M. Guelbenzú, I. Don Manuel, F. Caballero, E. Pardo Bazàn, 2021 (Niveau 3)
- *Lazarillo de Tormes*, 2022 (Niveau 1)

en **anglais** :

- *For Love and Dollars*, O. Henry, 2016 (Niveau 1)
- *Horror Stories*, E. Allan Poe, F. Marion Crawford, Saki, 2016 (Niveau 3)
- *Mr. Holmes*, Sir A. Conan Doyle, 2017 (Niveau 2)
- *Exile*, E. M. Eaton, D.H. Lawrence, G. Moore, 2018 (Niveau 3)
- *Tragedies, Tales from Shakespeare* de C. et M. Lamb, 2019 (Niveau 4)
- *Comedies, Tales from Shakespeare* de C. et M. Lamb, 2020 (Niveau 4)
- *Sherlock in Love*, Sir A. Conan Doyle, 2021 (Niveau 2)
- *Marriage Material*, Virginia Woolf, 2021 (Niveau 4)
- *Meandering Thoughts*, James Joyce, Katherine Mansfield, Virginia Woolf, 2021 (Niveau 4)

en **allemand** :

- *Histoires faciles à lire - allemand*, J. Rosler, K. Held, H. Spoerl, W. Breinholst, S. Von Radecki, C. Lemon, 2004
- *Über Stock und Stein*, Grimm, de H. Fallada, K. Tucholsky, 2018 (Niveau 3)
- *Lustige Geschichten*, J. H. Rösler, 2019 (Niveau 2)
- *Jugendgeschichten*, S. Zweig, H. Fallada, J. Roth, G. Grass et W. Schnurre, 2021 (Niveau 3)
- *Im Café*, C.S. Mahrendorff, S. Zweig, J. Roth, I. Morgner, E. M. Remarque, D. Glattauer, 2022 (Niveau 4)

en **russe** :

- *Premier amour*, Z. Hippius, A. Kouprine, A. Tchekhov, L. Tolstoï, 2018 (Niveau 2)

- *Histoires drôles*, V. Veressaïev, Ilf et Petrov, A. Avertchenko, D. Kharms, A. Kouprine, A. Tchekhov, 2019 (Niveau 2)
- *Histoires d'horreur*, V. Brioussov, A. Grine, O. Somov, I. Tourgueniev, 2020 (Niveau 3)
- *Mieux vaut en rire,* 6 nouvelles d'Ilf et Petrov, 2021 (Niveau 3)

en **grec** :
- *Voyou*, P. Delta, 2018 (Niveau 3)
- *La mer*, A. Karkavitsas, C. Théotokis, A. Papadiamándis, 2019 (Niveau 2)
- *Dieux blessés*, K. Karyotakis et M. Polydouri, 2020 (Niveau 3)

en **italien** :
- *Vampiri*, L. Capuana, D. O. Marrama, 2019 (Niveau 3)
- *Possessioni*, I. U. Tarchetti, A. Albertazzi, 2020 (Niveau 3)

en **portugais** :
- *Histórias de amores contrariados*, E. de Queiroz, 2020 (Niveau 3)

en **catalan** :
- *Ciutat i prodigis*, N. Oller, 2019 (Niveau 2)

en **japonais** :
- *Gōshu le viloncelliste et autres histoires d'animaux*, K. Miyazawa, 2021 (Niveau 3)
- *Contes d'autrefois*, J. Abe, 2022 (Niveau 1)

en **chinois** :
- *Herbes sauvages*, L. Xun, 2020 (Niveau 3)

en **polonais** :
- *Opowieści o miłości i rozpaczy*, B. Prus et E. Orzeszkowa, 2022 (Niveau 3)

en **tchèque** :
- *Výlet do Prahy*, K. Čapek, S. Čech, J. Hašek, A. Jirásek, J. Neruda et K. Notaro, 2022 (Niveau 3)

en **danois** :
- *Familiedramaet om den mørkerøde Fiat Ritmo*, E. Jepsen, 2022 (Niveau 3)

en **hébreu** :
- *Le petit oiseau et autres fantaisies*, H. Levin, 2022 (Niveau 3)

TABLE DES MATIÈRES

INTRODUCTION

Ce qu'il est coutume d'appeler « l'âge du jazz » aux États-Unis correspond à l'Amérique des années 1920, une période d'insouciance et d'excès que Francis Scott Fitzgerald a su décrire dans *Les contes de l'âge du Jazz* dont est tiré « L'étrange histoire de Benjamin Button ». Derrière les excès et l'insouciance, se cache également un cadre rigide, crispé sur certaines conventions sociales, centré sur le profil « WASP » (*White Anglo-Saxon Protestant*), et peu ouvert à ce qui lui était étranger. Cette dimension sociale et politique n'est qu'esquissée, par touches impressionnistes, en toile de fond de cette histoire – cette curieuse histoire de Benjamin Button, qui est bel et bien étrange.

On cherchera vainement une morale dans ce conte car le sens profond de ce texte se trouve dans les questions qu'il pose. Il nous demande tout d'abord d'accepter l'invraisemblable, voire l'impossible : commencer sa vie par la fin, la finir par le début. C'est à travers le décalage entre Benjamin Button et le reste des personnages que le lecteur découvre, sous un jour nouveau, le monde qui l'entoure. Riche en émotions et en situations farfelues, le récit s'enrichit au fil des lectures : Francis Scott Fitzgerald n'a laissé aucun détail au hasard, si bien qu'il ne manque pas, au détour d'un mot ou d'une expression, de souligner certaines caractéristiques de cet âge du jazz : une génération marquée par la guerre, par l'hypocrisie de la prohibition et par le développement de la société de consommation où l'argent est roi.

À travers ce conte, Francis Scott Fitzgerald dresse le portrait d'une société qui régresse, à l'image de ce personnage qui ne parvient plus à comprendre ce qui l'entoure et à qui les mots finissent par manquer.

- **make it to** = réussir à rejoindre
- **served** = servir (dans l'armée)
- **disappointed him** = l'ont déçu

- **a lasting effect** = un effet durable
- **the tantalizing impression** = l'impression d'être si prêt de

- **breakdowns** = dépressions nerveuses

- **an old flame** = un amour de jeunesse
- **cruelty of wealth** = cruauté de l'opulence
- **depict** = décrivent

ABOUT THE AUTHOR

Francis Scott Fitzgerald was born in St Paul, Minnesota in 1896. He attended Princeton University, which he left in 1917, without finishing in 1917, disappointed that he could not make it to the football team of the university and therefore decided to join the army, which he served from 1917 to 1919, which also disappointed him in that they did not send him overseas. These two experiences had a lasting effect on Fitzgerald, as he later confessed: they had the tantalizing impression of being about to be successful, without actually reaching this success.

In 1920, he married Zelda Sayre, with whom he would spend the rest of his life and who would have an important influence on his writing. They led a tumultuous life first in New York, then in France, where he joined other American expatriates (Ernest Hemingway, John Dos Passos or Gertrude Stein). However, Fitzgerald's life was deeply affected by Zelda's numerous breakdowns.

He published *This side of Paradise* and his first collection of short stories in 1920. Two years later, he published a second collection of short stories: *Tales of the Jazz Age*. His real success came with the publication of *The Great Gatsby* in 1925, about Gatsby's pursuit of an old flame, crushed by the cruelty of wealth.

His novels and short stories depict the USA in the 1920s, what is called the Jazz age: a time of frivolity for a sophisticated youth.

Les 10 mots clés

a custom = une coutume
howls = des cris
a crib = un berceau
shame = la honte
gloom = l'obscurité
the forehead = le front
a mishap = une mésaventure
appalled = horrifié
hushed = à mi-voix
a blanket = une couverture

Part I

The first days of new-born baby are not easy: the baby discovers the world, his parents and society. But what if the baby is a very old man? How could his father react? How to cope with such an impossible situation?

The disclosure of this challenge makes us ponder about the way we expect others to behave…

~

- **it was the proper thing to** = il était bien vu de
- **so I'm told** = à ce que l'on m'a dit
- **decreed** = décrété
- **uttered** = prononcés
- **anaesthetic** = aseptisé

- **bearing upon** = une incidence sur
- **astonishing** = étonnante
- **set down** = raconter

- **ante-bellum** = d'avant la guerre de sécession (1861-1865)

- **peerage** = noblesse
- **custom** = coutume

- **cuff** = manchette

I

As long ago as 1860 it was the proper thing to be born at home. At present, so I am told, the high gods of medicine have decreed that the first cries of the young shall be uttered upon the anaesthetic air of a hospital, preferably a fashionable one. So young Mr. and Mrs. Roger Button were fifty years ahead of style when they decided, one day in the summer of 1860, that their first baby should be born in a hospital. Whether this anachronism had any bearing upon the astonishing history I am about to set down will never be known.

I shall tell you what occurred, and let you judge for yourself.

The Roger Buttons held an enviable position, both social and financial, in ante-bellum Baltimore. They were related to the This Family and the That Family, which, as every Southerner knew, entitled them to membership in that enormous peerage which largely populated the Confederacy. This was their first experience with the charming old custom of having babies—Mr. Button was naturally nervous. He hoped it would be a boy so that he could be sent to Yale College in Connecticut, at which institution Mr. Button himself had been known for four years by the somewhat obvious nickname of "Cuff."

- **arose** = se leva
- **stock** = nœud de cravate

- **had borne in new life upon its bosom** = avait apporté une nouvelle vie sur son sein

- **physician** = médecin

- **unwritten ethics** = éthique tacite

- **picturesque** = pittoresque

- **faced around** = se tourna vers lui
- **settling** = se dessinant

- **a gasping rush** = hors d'haleine

- **Talk sense!** = Parlez de manière sensée !
- **sharply** = durement

On the September morning consecrated to the enormous event he arose nervously at six o'clock, dressed himself, adjusted an impeccable stock, and hurried forth through the streets of Baltimore to the hospital, to determine whether the darkness of the night had borne in new life upon its bosom.

When he was approximately a hundred yards from the Maryland Private Hospital for Ladies and Gentlemen he saw Doctor Keene, the family physician, descending the front steps, rubbing his hands together with a washing movement—as all doctors are required to do by the unwritten ethics of their profession.

Mr. Roger Button, the president of Roger Button & Co., Wholesale Hardware, began to run toward Doctor Keene with much less dignity than was expected from a Southern gentleman of that picturesque period. "Doctor Keene!" he called. "Oh, Doctor Keene!"

The doctor heard him, faced around, and stood waiting, a curious expression settling on his harsh, medicinal face as Mr. Button drew near.

"What happened?" demanded Mr. Button, as he came up in a gasping rush. "What was it? How is she? A boy? Who is it? What—"

"Talk sense!" said Doctor Keene sharply. He appeared

- **begged** = implora

- **frowned** = fronça les sourcils
- **after a fashion** = dans un certain sens
- **glance** = regard

- **Here now!** = Écoutez !

- **snapped [...] out** = lâcha avec violence
- **muttering** = grommelant

- **appalled** = horrifié

- **cuttingly** = sèchement
- **what's more** = du reste

- **I'm through** = j'en ai fini

somewhat irritated.

"Is the child born?" begged Mr. Button.

Doctor Keene frowned. "Why, yes, I suppose so—after a fashion." Again he threw a curious glance at Mr. Button.

"Is my wife all right?"

"Yes."

"Is it a boy or a girl?"

"Here now!" cried Doctor Keene in a perfect passion of irritation, "I'll ask you to go and see for yourself. Outrageous!" He snapped the last word out in almost one syllable, then he turned away muttering: "Do you imagine a case like this will help my professional reputation? One more would ruin me—ruin anybody."

"What's the matter?" demanded Mr. Button appalled. "Triplets?"

"No, not triplets!" answered the doctor cuttingly. "What's more, you can go and see for yourself. And get another doctor. I brought you into the world, young man, and I've been physician to your family for forty years, but I'm through with you! I don't want to see

- **sharply** = brusquement
- **phaeton** = phaéton (*automobile du début du* XXe *s.*)
- **curbstone** = trottoir
- **severely** = l'air grave

- **mishap** = mésaventure
- **had occured** = s'était produit

- **gloom** = obscurité
- **swallowing his shame** = ravalant sa honte

- **utter** = absolue
- **spread itself** = se repandit sur

you or any of your relatives ever again! Good-bye!"

Then he turned sharply, and without another word climbed into his phaeton, which was waiting at the curbstone, and drove severely away.

Mr. Button stood there upon the sidewalk, stupefied and trembling from head to foot. What horrible mishap had occurred? He had suddenly lost all desire to go into the Maryland Private Hospital for Ladies and Gentlemen—it was with the greatest difficulty that, a moment later, he forced himself to mount the steps and enter the front door.

A nurse was sitting behind a desk in the opaque gloom of the hall. Swallowing his shame, Mr. Button approached her.

"Good-morning," she remarked, looking up at him pleasantly.

"Good-morning. I—I am Mr. Button."

At this a look of utter terror spread itself over the girl's face. She rose to her feet and seemed about to fly from the hall, restraining herself only with the most apparent difficulty.

"I want to see my child," said Mr. Button.

- **bathed** = baigné
- **perspiration** = sueur
- **falteringly** = d'un pas mal assuré

- **Clank!** = Bing !
- **clattered** = tomba bruyamment

- **shrieked** = hurla
- **on the verge of** = sur le point de

- **hearty contempt** = mépris absolu

- **hushed** = à mi-voix

- **hoarsely** = d'une voix rauque

The nurse gave a little scream. "Oh—of course!" she cried hysterically. "Upstairs. Right upstairs. Go—*up!*"

She pointed the direction, and Mr. Button, bathed in cool perspiration, turned falteringly, and began to mount to the second floor. In the upper hall he addressed another nurse who approached him, basin in hand. "I'm Mr. Button," he managed to articulate. "I want to see my——"

Clank! The basin clattered to the floor and rolled in the direction of the stairs. Clank! Clank! It began a methodical descent as if sharing in the general terror which this gentleman provoked.

"I want to see my child!" Mr. Button almost shrieked. He was on the verge of collapse.

Clank! The basin reached the first floor. The nurse regained control of herself, and threw Mr. Button a look of hearty contempt.

"All *right*, Mr. Button," she agreed in a hushed voice. "Very *well!* But if you *knew* what a state it's put us all in this morning! It's perfectly outrageous! The hospital will never have a ghost of a reputation after——"

"Hurry!" he cried hoarsely. "I can't stand this!"

- **dragged** = traina les pieds
- **proceeded** = s'élevaient
- **howls** = cris
- **in later parlance** = qu'on appellerait plus tard
- **crying-room** = chambre des pleurs

- **gasped** = s'exclama

- **wrapped** = enveloppé
- **crammed into** = fourré dans
- **cribs** = berceau
- **sparse** = clairsemé
- **dripped** = dégoulinait
- **beard** = barbe
- **waved** = ondoyait
- **fanned** = se balançait
- **dim, faded eyes** = regard éteint, passé
- **lurked** = laissait deviner
- **puzzled** = perplexe
- **ghastly** = horrible

"Come this way, then, Mr. Button."

He dragged himself after her. At the end of a long hall they reached a room from which proceeded a variety of howls—indeed, a room which, in later parlance, would have been known as the "crying-room." They entered.

"Well," gasped Mr. Button, "which is mine?"

"There!" said the nurse.

Mr. Button's eyes followed her pointing finger, and this is what he saw. Wrapped in a voluminous white blanket, and partly crammed into one of the cribs, there sat an old man apparently about seventy years of age. His sparse hair was almost white, and from his chin dripped a long smoke-coloured beard, which waved absurdly back and forth, fanned by the breeze coming in at the window. He looked up at Mr. Button with dim, faded eyes in which lurked a puzzled question.

"Am I mad?" thundered Mr. Button, his terror resolving into rage. "Is this some ghastly hospital joke?

"It doesn't seem like a joke to us," replied the nurse severely. "And I don't know whether you're mad or not—but that is most certainly your child."

- **forehead** = front

- **threescore and ten** = soixante-dix ans
- **hung over**= retombaient
- **crib** = berceau

- **placidly** = avec placidité
- **cracked** = fêlée

- **started** = sursautèrent

- **querulously** = d'un ton grincheux

- **burst out** = explosa
- **frantically** = hors de lui

- **whine** = geignard

- **wearily** = avec lassitude

- **why don't you** = si vous le voulez bien

The cool perspiration redoubled on Mr. Button's forehead. He closed his eyes, and then, opening them, looked again. There was no mistake—he was gazing at a man of threescore and ten—a *baby* of threescore and ten, a baby whose feet hung over the sides of the crib in which it was reposing.

The old man looked placidly from one to the other for a moment, and then suddenly spoke in a cracked and ancient voice. "Are you my father?" he demanded.

Mr. Button and the nurse started violently.

"Because if you are," went on the old man querulously, "I wish you'd get me out of this place—or, at least, get them to put a comfortable rocker in here."

"Where in God's name did you come from? Who are you?" burst out Mr. Button frantically.

"I can't tell you *exactly* who I am," replied the querulous whine, "because I've only been born a few hours—but my last name is certainly Button."

"You lie! You're an impostor!"

The old man turned wearily to the nurse. "Nice way to welcome a new-born child," he complained in a weak voice. "Tell him he's wrong, why don't you?"

- **incredulously** = d'un air incrédule

- **youngster of quiet tastes** = jeune qui aime la tranquilité
- **yelling and howling** = cris et hurlements
- **I haven't been able to get a wink of sleep** = je n'ai pas pu fermer l'oeil
- **shrill** = aiguë

- **sank down** = se laissa tomber
- **My heavens!** = Mon dieu !

- **dreadful** = affreuse

- **crowded** = plein de monde
- **stalking** = suivant partout

"You're wrong, Mr. Button," said the nurse severely. "This is your child, and you'll have to make the best of it. We're going to ask you to take him home with you as soon as possible—some time to-day."

"Home?" repeated Mr. Button incredulously.

"Yes, we can't have him here. We really can't, you know?"

"I'm right glad of it," whined the old man. "This is a fine place to keep a youngster of quiet tastes. With all this yelling and howling, I haven't been able to get a wink of sleep. I asked for something to eat"—here his voice rose to a shrill note of protest—"and they brought me a bottle of milk!"

Mr. Button, sank down upon a chair near his son and concealed his face in his hands. "My heavens!" he murmured, in an ecstasy of horror. "What will people say? What must I do?"

"You'll have to take him home," insisted the nurse—"immediately!"

A grotesque picture formed itself with dreadful clarity before the eyes of the tortured man—a picture of himself walking through the crowded streets of the city with this appalling apparition stalking by his side.

- **moaned** = gémit

- **plod on** = marcheraient d'un pas lourd
- **bustling stores** = magasins bondés

- **Pull yourself together** = Reprenez-vous

- **crackle** = gloussement
- **swaddling garment** = lange
- **quavered** = dit d'une voix chevrotante

- **primly** = d'un ton guindé

- **itches** = me gratte

“I can’t. I can’t,” he moaned.

People would stop to speak to him, and what was he going to say? He would have to introduce this—this septuagenarian: “This is my son, born early this morning.” And then the old man would gather his blanket around him and they would plod on, past the bustling stores, the slave market—for a dark instant Mr. Button wished passionately that his son was black—past the luxurious houses of the residential district, past the home for the aged....

“Come! Pull yourself together,” commanded the nurse.

“See here,” the old man announced suddenly, “if you think I’m going to walk home in this blanket, you’re entirely mistaken.”

“Babies always have blankets.”

With a malicious crackle the old man held up a small white swaddling garment. “Look!” he quavered. “*This* is what they had ready for me.”

“Babies always wear those,” said the nurse primly.

“Well,” said the old man, “this baby’s not going to wear anything in about two minutes. This blanket itches. They might at least have given me a sheet.”

- **banged** = claqua
- **savagely** = sauvagement

"Keep it on! Keep it on!" said Mr. Button hurriedly. He turned to the nurse. "What'll I do?"

"Go down town and buy your son some clothes."

Mr. Button's son's voice followed him down into the hall: "And a cane, father. I want to have a cane."

Mr. Button banged the outer door savagely....

~

COMPREHENSION

1. Who are the following characters? (6 points)

a) Roger Button
b) Doctor Keene
c) Benjamin Button

2. Quiz (10 points)

A – How does Doctor Keene welcome Roger Button?

a) He is enthusiastic.
b) He is eager to speak about the baby.
c) He is cold and angry.
d) He wants to be there when Mr Button meets his child.

B – What is Roger Button's reaction when he sees his son?

a) He feels pity.
b) He feels surprised.
c) He feels angry.
d) He feels tired.

C – Mr. Button's child is different from the other babies because...

a) ...he is very small.
b) ...he looks like his mother.
c) ...he has the appearance of an old man.
d) ...he already has many friends.

D – The child is...
a) ...happy to see his father.
b) ...eager to get home.
c) ...grumpy and rude.

E – The child asks his father for...
a) ...a cane.
b) ...a toy.
c) ...a friend.
d) ...a nurse.

EXPRESSION

Imagine you are the nurse and you write on your diary the entry for the day Benjamin Button was born. (4 pts)

Les 10 mots clés

a clerk = un commis
to conceal = dissimuler
a fancy dress = tenue de soirée
to spank = donner la fessée
shears = des ciseaux
dyed = teint
aged stoop = voûté par l'âge
a rattle = un hochet
unexpectedly = à l'improviste
spectacles = des lunettes

Parts II and III

An old man in babies' clothes… What is he to do? How to behave like a baby when your interest lies in grown-ups' activities? —an unusual situation that the Button family has to face.

~

- **clerk** = commis

- **without due consideration** = sans réfléchir

- **babies' supply department** = le rayon layette
- **rear** = au fond (du magasin)

- **unusually** = inhabituelle

- **inquired** = s'enquit
- **shifting his ground** = changeant sa tactique
- **scent** = deviner

- **cut off** = couper
- **dye** = teindre

II

"Good-morning," Mr. Button said nervously, to the clerk in the Chesapeake Dry Goods Company. "I want to buy some clothes for my child."

"How old is your child, sir?"

"About six hours," answered Mr. Button, without due consideration.

"Babies' supply department in the rear."

"Why, I don't think—I'm not sure that's what I want. It's—he's an unusually large-size child. Exceptionally—ah large."

"They have the largest child's sizes."

"Where is the boys' department?" inquired Mr. Button, shifting his ground desperately. He felt that the clerk must surely scent his shameful secret.

"Right here."

"Well——" He hesitated. The notion of dressing his son in men's clothes was repugnant to him. If, say, he could only find a very large boy's suit, he might cut off that long and awful beard, dye the white hair brown,

- **conceal** = dissimuler
- **retain** = conserver

- **frantic** = frénétique
- **revealed** = révéla

- **aisle** = rayon

- **brightened** = illuminé
- **toward** = en direction de
- **dummy** = mannequin

- **stared** = regarda avec attention
- **fancy dress** = tenue de soirée

- **wrap it up** = emballez-le

and thus manage to conceal the worst, and to retain something of his own self-respect—not to mention his position in Baltimore society.

But a frantic inspection of the boys' department revealed no suits to fit the new-born Button. He blamed the store, of course—in such cases it is the thing to blame the store.

"How old did you say that boy of yours was?" demanded the clerk curiously.

"He's—sixteen."

"Oh, I beg your pardon. I thought you said six *hours*. You'll find the youths' department in the next aisle."

Mr. Button turned miserably away. Then he stopped, brightened, and pointed his finger toward a dressed dummy in the window display. "There!" he exclaimed. "I'll take that suit, out there on the dummy."

The clerk stared. "Why," he protested, "that's not a child's suit. At least it *is*, but it's for fancy dress. You could wear it yourself!"

"Wrap it up," insisted his customer nervously. "That's what I want."

- **snapped out** = il lui lança, sèchement

- **with a quizzical eye** = d'un oeil perplexe

- **be made a monkey of** = qu'on se moque de moi

- **fiercely** = avec férocité
- **spank** = donner la fessée
- **swallowed** = déglutit
- **penultimate** = avant-dernier

- **start** = sursauter

The astonished clerk obeyed.

Back at the hospital Mr. Button entered the nursery and almost threw the package at his son. "Here's your clothes," he snapped out.

The old man untied the package and viewed the contents with a quizzical eye.

"They look sort of funny to me," he complained, "I don't want to be made a monkey of—"

"You've made a monkey of me!" retorted Mr. Button fiercely. "Never you mind how funny you look. Put them on—or I'll—or I'll *spank* you." He swallowed uneasily at the penultimate word, feeling nevertheless that it was the proper thing to say.

"All right, father"—this with a grotesque simulation of filial respect—"you've lived longer; you know best. Just as you say."

As before, the sound of the word "father" caused Mr. Button to start violently.

"And hurry."

"I'm hurrying, father."

- **dotted** = à pois

- **over the latter waved** = sur ce dernier ondoyait
- **drooping** = pendait
- **waist** = la taille

- **shears** = ciseaux

- **fell far short** = était loin d'être
- **scraggly** = ébouriffé
- **watery** = larmoyants
- **oddly** = étrangement
- **obdurate** = osbtiné
- **sternly** = sévèrement

- **trustingly** = confiant
- **quavered** = il chevrota

- **grunted** = grommela
- **Methuselah** = Mathusalem (*figure biblique censée avoir vécu près de mille ans*)

When his son was dressed Mr. Button regarded him with depression. The costume consisted of dotted socks, pink pants, and a belted blouse with a wide white collar. Over the latter waved the long whitish beard, drooping almost to the waist. The effect was not good.

"Wait!"

Mr. Button seized a hospital shears and with three quick snaps amputated a large section of the beard. But even with this improvement the ensemble fell far short of perfection. The remaining brush of scraggly hair, the watery eyes, the ancient teeth, seemed oddly out of tone with the gaiety of the costume. Mr. Button, however, was obdurate—he held out his hand. "Come along!" he said sternly.

His son took the hand trustingly. "What are you going to call me, dad?" he quavered as they walked from the nursery—"just 'baby' for a while? till you think of a better name?"

Mr. Button grunted. "I don't know," he answered harshly. "I think we'll call you Methuselah."

- **dyed** = teint
- **sparse** = clairsemé
- **glistened** = luisait
- **flabbergasted** = sidéré
- **a poor excuse** = une mauvaise excuse
- **aged stoop** = voûté par l'âge

- **invidious** = peu enviable

- **clipping and dyeing** = taille et teinture
- **faded** = passé

- **unwavering** = inébranlable

- **prevailed upon** = se laissa fléchir
- **oatmeal** = porridge
- **rattle** = hochet
- **in no uncertain terms** = expressément
- **weary expression** = air las
- **jingling** = le faire cliqueter
- **at intervals** = à intervalles réguliers

III

Even after the new addition to the Button family had had his hair cut short and then dyed to a sparse unnatural black, had had his face shaved so close that it glistened, and had been attired in small-boy clothes made to order by a flabbergasted tailor, it was impossible for Button to ignore the fact that his son was a poor excuse for a first family baby. Despite his aged stoop, Benjamin Button—for it was by this name they called him instead of by the appropriate but invidious Methuselah—was five feet eight inches tall. His clothes did not conceal this, nor did the clipping and dyeing of his eyebrows disguise the fact that the eyes underneath were faded and watery and tired. In fact, the baby-nurse who had been engaged in advance left the house after one look, in a state of considerable indignation.

But Mr. Button persisted in his unwavering purpose. Benjamin was a baby, and a baby he should remain. At first he declared that if Benjamin didn't like warm milk he could go without food altogether, but he was finally prevailed upon to allow his son bread and butter, and even oatmeal by way of a compromise. One day he brought home a rattle and, giving it to Benjamin, insisted in no uncertain terms that he should "play with it," whereupon the old man took it with a weary expression and could be heard jingling it obediently at intervals throughout the day.

- **soothing** = apaisants

- **unexpectedly** = à l'improviste
- **faint** = légère
- **haze** = fumée
- **butt** = mégot
- **dark havana** = cigare de la havane de couleur sombre

- **stunt his growth** = retarder sa croissance

- **lead** = de plomb
- **to perfect** = pour parfaire

- **steal down**= descendait discrètement

- **pore** = se plonger
- **cotton cows** = vaches en tissu
- **stubbornness** = entêtement
- **were of little avail** = ne servaient pas à grand-chose

There can be no doubt, though, that the rattle bored him, and that he found other and more soothing amusements when he was left alone. For instance, Mr. Button discovered one day that during the preceding week he had smoked more cigars than ever before—a phenomenon, which was explained a few days later when, entering the nursery unexpectedly, he found the room full of faint blue haze and Benjamin, with a guilty expression on his face, trying to conceal the butt of a dark Havana. This, of course, called for a severe spanking, but Mr. Button found that he could not bring himself to administer it. He merely warned his son that he would "stunt his growth."

Nevertheless he persisted in his attitude. He brought home lead soldiers, he brought toy trains, he brought large pleasant animals made of cotton, and, to perfect the illusion which he was creating—for himself at least—he passionately demanded of the clerk in the toy-store whether "the paint would come off the pink duck if the baby put it in his mouth." But, despite all his father's efforts, Benjamin refused to be interested. He would steal down the back stairs and return to the nursery with a volume of the Encyclopedia Britannica, over which he would pore through an afternoon, while his cotton cows and his Noah's ark were left neglected on the floor. Against such a stubbornness Mr. Button's efforts were of little avail.

- **sensation** = succès fulgurant
- **mishap** = mésaventure
- **kinsfolk** = leur famille
- **Civil War** = la guerre de Sécession

- **unfailingly** = inlassablement
- **racked their brains** = se creusaient la tête
- **device** = astuce

- **decay** = déclin

- **stiff-joined** = courbaturé
- **tops and marbles** = toupies et billes

- **sling shot** = lance-pierre
- **a feat** = un exploit

- **contrived** = trouva le moyen de

- **were expected of him** = étaient attendues de sa part
- **obliging** = obligeant

- **antagonism** = hostilité
- **wore off** = s'atténua

The sensation created in Baltimore was, at first, prodigious. What the mishap would have cost the Buttons and their kinsfolk socially cannot be determined, for the outbreak of the Civil War drew the city's attention to other things. A few people who were unfailingly polite racked their brains for compliments to give to the parents—and finally hit upon the ingenious device of declaring that the baby resembled his grandfather, a fact which, due to the standard state of decay common to all men of seventy, could not be denied. Mr. and Mrs. Roger Button were not pleased, and Benjamin's grandfather was furiously insulted.

Benjamin, once he left the hospital, took life as he found it. Several small boys were brought to see him, and he spent a stiff-jointed afternoon trying to work up an interest in tops and marbles—he even managed, quite accidentally, to break a kitchen window with a stone from a sling shot, a feat which secretly delighted his father.

Thereafter Benjamin contrived to break something every day, but he did these things only because they were expected of him, and because he was by nature obliging.

When his grandfather's initial antagonism wore off, Benjamin and that gentleman took enormous pleasure in one another's company. They would sit for hours,

- **cronies** = camarades
- **at ease** = à l'aise

- **in awe** = intimidés

- **puzzled** = perplexe

- **read up on it** = lut des articles à ce sujet

- **urging** = insistance
- **milder** = plus calmes

- **knit** = se ressouder

- **kindergarten** = jardin d'enfants
- **pasting** = coller
- **weaving** = tisser

- **drowse off** = s'assoupir

these two, so far apart in age and experience, and, like old cronies, discuss with tireless monotony the slow events of the day. Benjamin felt more at ease in his grandfather's presence than in his parents'—they seemed always somewhat in awe of him and, despite the dictatorial authority they exercised over him, frequently addressed him as "Mr."

He was as puzzled as any one else at the apparently advanced age of his mind and body at birth. He read up on it in the medical journal, but found that no such case had been previously recorded. At his father's urging he made an honest attempt to play with other boys, and frequently he joined in the milder games—football shook him up too much, and he feared that in case of a fracture his ancient bones would refuse to knit.

When he was five he was sent to kindergarten, where he was initiated into the art of pasting green paper on orange paper, of weaving coloured maps and manufacturing eternal cardboard necklaces. He was inclined to drowse off to sleep in the middle of these tasks, a habit which both irritated and frightened his young teacher. To his relief she complained to his parents, and he was removed from the school. The Roger Buttons told their friends that they felt he was too young.

- **custom** = coutume

- **deceive** = trahissaient
- **iron-gray** = gris argenté
- **concealing dye** = teinture dissimulante

- **ruddy** = rose
- **He could not tell.** = Il n'aurait pu le dire.
- **stooped** = voûté

- **scarcely dared** = n'osait à peine

By the time he was twelve years old his parents had grown used to him. Indeed, so strong is the force of custom that they no longer felt that he was different from any other child—except when some curious anomaly reminded them of the fact. But one day a few weeks after his twelfth birthday, while looking in the mirror, Benjamin made, or thought he made, an astonishing discovery. Did his eyes deceive him, or had his hair turned in the dozen years of his life from white to iron-gray under its concealing dye? Was the network of wrinkles on his face becoming less pronounced? Was his skin healthier and firmer, with even a touch of ruddy winter colour? He could not tell. He knew that he no longer stooped, and that his physical condition had improved since the early days of his life.

"Can it be——?" he thought to himself, or, rather, scarcely dared to think.

He went to his father. "I am grown," he announced determinedly. "I want to put on long trousers."

His father hesitated. "Well," he said finally, "I don't know. Fourteen is the age for putting on long trousers—and you are only twelve."

"But you'll have to admit," protested Benjamin, "that I'm big for my age."

- **with illusory speculation** = en faisant semblant de réfléchir

- **was to** = devait

- **spectacles** = lunettes
- **in return for** = en échange de
- **suit of** = ensemble de

His father looked at him with illusory speculation. "Oh, I'm not so sure of that," he said. "I was as big as you when I was twelve."

This was not true—it was all part of Roger Button's silent agreement with himself to believe in his son's normality.

Finally a compromise was reached. Benjamin was to continue to dye his hair. He was to make a better attempt to play with boys of his own age. He was not to wear his spectacles or carry a cane in the street. In return for these concessions he was allowed his first suit of long trousers...

~

COMPREHENSION

1. Quiz (6 pts)

A – Why is it difficult for Benjamin's father to buy clothes for him?

a) Because the clothes are expensive.
b) Because they are too small for Benjamin.
c) Because none of the clothes are for new-borns.
d) Because Benjamin's father does not know how to choose.

B – Why did Benjamin break something every day?

a) Because he enjoyed doing it.
b) Because he could not help it.
c) Because that was what children do.
d) Because he was angry.

C – Benjamin Button was not allowed...

a) ...to dye his hair.
b) ...to question his father's orders.
c) ...to play with boys his own age.
d) ...to wear his spectacles or carry a cane in the street.

2. True or false? (6 pts)

A – Knowing Benjamin Button better...

a) Benjamin Button feels deep respect for his father.
b) Benjamin Button cut his beard and dyed his hair.
c) Benjamin Button's real name is Methuselah.
d) His favourite meal is oatmeal.

B – What are Benjamin Button's favourite hobbies?

a) Playing with a little train
b) Playing with a rattle
c) Reading the Encyclopaedia Brittanica
d) Smoking cigars

C – What happened shortly after his twelfth birthday?

a) He was allowed to use his cane outside.
b) He started to enjoy playing with friends of his age.
c) He discovered that he was getting younger.
d) He understood that would remain old all his life.

EXPRESSION

1. Write a short portrait of Benjamin Button as a child. (4 pts)
2. Explain why Benjamin Button is different from the other children. (4 pts)

Les 10 mots clés

a freshman = un étudiant en première année
wearily = avec lassitude
to be fated = que le sort en ait décidé
a gait = une démarche
a phaeton = un phaéton (*automobile du début du XX*[e] *s.*)
gorgeous = magnifique
dry-goods = de la quincaillerie
glittering = scintillant
a buggy = un boghei (*petit cabriolet découvert*)
to yawn = bâiller

Parts IV and V

Time to go to school, to university and to find a job for Benjamin Button: nothing goes as expected, as usual. The world is not ready to accept Benjamin. Nothing better than the family business to find one's place and meet new people…

~

- **suffice to** = il suffit de
- **ungrowth** = décroissance
- **erect** = droit

- **cracked quaver** = aspect cassé et chevrotant

- **freshman class** = première année de l'université

- **matriculation** = inscription

- **registrar** = responsable de la scolarité
- **glancing** = jetant un coup d'oeil
- **dye** = teinture
- **disclosed** = révéla

- **due at** = était attendu
- **seemed to be no help for it** = il ne pouvait rien y faire

- **inquire about** = vous renseigner au sujet de

IV

Of the life of Benjamin Button between his twelfth and twenty-first year I intend to say little. Suffice to record that they were years of normal ungrowth. When Benjamin was eighteen he was erect as a man of fifty; he had more hair and it was of a dark gray; his step was firm, his voice had lost its cracked quaver and descended to a healthy baritone. So his father sent him up to Connecticut to take examinations for entrance to Yale College. Benjamin passed his examination and became a member of the freshman class.

On the third day following his matriculation he received a notification from Mr. Hart, the college registrar, to call at his office and arrange his schedule. Benjamin, glancing in the mirror, decided that his hair needed a new application of its brown dye, but an anxious inspection of his bureau drawer disclosed that the dye bottle was not there. Then he remembered—he had emptied it the day before and thrown it away.

He was in a dilemma. He was due at the registrar's in five minutes. There seemed to be no help for it—he must go as he was. He did.

"Good-morning," said the registrar politely. "You've come to inquire about your son."

- **cut him off** = l'interrompit

- **I'm expecting** = j'attends

- **freshman** = étudiant en première année

- **frowned** = fronça les sourcils
- **glanced** = jeta un regard

- **flushing slightly** = rougissant légèrement

- **wearily** = avec lassitude

- **sternly** = d'un air sévère

"Why, as a matter of fact, my name's Button——" began Benjamin, but Mr. Hart cut him off.

"I'm very glad to meet you, Mr. Button. I'm expecting your son here any minute."

"That's me!" burst out Benjamin. "I'm a freshman."

"What!"

"I'm a freshman."

"Surely you're joking."

"Not at all."

The registrar frowned and glanced at a card before him. "Why, I have Mr. Benjamin Button's age down here as eighteen."

"That's my age," asserted Benjamin, flushing slightly.

The registrar eyed him wearily. "Now surely, Mr. Button, you don't expect me to believe that."

Benjamin smiled wearily. "I am eighteen," he repeated.

The registrar pointed sternly to the door. "Get out," he said. "Get out of college and get out of town. You are

- **lunatic** = fou

- **undergraduates** = étudiants de licence

- **a little way** = quelques pas
- **infuriated** = furieux
- **doorway** = devant

- **a chorus of titters** = un chœur de gloussements

- **was not fated** = le sort décida que

- **swarm** = essaim

- **word had gone around** = the bruit avait couru que

- **palm off** = se faire passer pour
- **permeated** = parcourait
- **hatless** = tête nue

a dangerous lunatic."

"I am eighteen."

Mr. Hart opened the door. "The idea!" he shouted. "A man of your age trying to enter here as a freshman. Eighteen years old, are you? Well, I'll give you eighteen minutes to get out of town."

Benjamin Button walked with dignity from the room, and half a dozen undergraduates, who were waiting in the hall, followed him curiously with their eyes. When he had gone a little way he turned around, faced the infuriated registrar, who was still standing in the doorway, and repeated in a firm voice: "I am eighteen years old."

To a chorus of titters which went up from the group of undergraduates, Benjamin walked away.

But he was not fated to escape so easily. On his melancholy walk to the railroad station he found that he was being followed by a group, then by a swarm, and finally by a dense mass of undergraduates. The word had gone around that a lunatic had passed the entrance examinations for Yale and attempted to palm himself off as a youth of eighteen. A fever of excitement permeated the college. Men ran hatless out of classes, the football team abandoned its practice

- **mob** = la foule
- **bonnets awry** = bonnets de travers
- **bustles** = crinolines elliptiques (*jupons à armatures flexibles*)
- **tender sensibilities** = douloureuse susceptibilité

- **the wandering jew** = le juif errant

- **prep school** = classe préparatoire

- **old men's home** = asile de vieillards

- **gait** = démarche

- **ill-considered taunts** = railleries inconsidérées

and joined the mob, professors' wives with bonnets awry and bustles out of position, ran shouting after the procession, from which proceeded a continual succession of remarks aimed at the tender sensibilities of Benjamin Button.

"He must be the wandering Jew!"

"He ought to go to prep school at his age!"

"Look at the infant prodigy!"

"He thought this was the old men's home."

"Go up to Harvard!"

Benjamin increased his gait, and soon he was running. He would show them! He *would* go to Harvard, and then they would regret these ill-considered taunts!

Safely on board the train for Baltimore, he put his head from the window. "You'll regret this!" he shouted.

"Ha-ha!" the undergraduates laughed. "Ha-ha-ha!" It was the biggest mistake that Yale College had ever made...

~

- **signalised** = marqua

- **that is** = c'est-à-dire

- **companionable** = s'entendaient

- **grayish** = grisonnant
- **passed for** = passer pour

- **phaeton** = phaéton (*automobile du début du xx*^{e} *s.*)
- **attired** = vêtus

- **gorgeous** = magnifique
- **drenched** = baignait
- **lustreless** = mate
- **motionless** = immobile
- **carpeted for rods of** = recouverte d'un tapis de
- **wheat** = blé
- **translucent** = translucide
- **sheer** = pure

- **dry-goods** = quincaillerie

V

In 1880 Benjamin Button was twenty years old, and he signalised his birthday by going to work for his father in Roger Button & Co., Wholesale Hardware. It was in that same year that he began "going out socially"—that is, his father insisted on taking him to several fashionable dances. Roger Button was now fifty, and he and his son were more and more companionable—in fact, since Benjamin had ceased to dye his hair (which was still grayish) they appeared about the same age, and could have passed for brothers.

One night in August they got into the phaeton attired in their full-dress suits and drove out to a dance at the Shevlins' country house, situated just outside of Baltimore. It was a gorgeous evening. A full moon drenched the road to the lustreless colour of platinum, and late-blooming harvest flowers breathed into the motionless air aromas that were like low, half-heard laughter. The open country, carpeted for rods around with bright wheat, was translucent as in the day. It was almost impossible not to be affected by the sheer beauty of the sky—almost.

"There's a great future in the dry-goods business," Roger Button was saying. He was not a spiritual man—his aesthetic sense was rudimentary.

- **tricks** = tours
- **youngsters** = les jeunes

- **drifted into view** = apparut
- **sighing sound that crept** = léger sifflement qui leur parvenait
- **rustle** = bruissement

- **brougham** = coupé de ville
- **disembarking** = descendaient

- **beautiful as sin** = qui avait la beauté du diable
- **started** = tressaillit
- **rigour** = une sensation de rigité

- **steady thumping** = battement régulier

- **slender and frail** = mince et frêle
- **ashen** = gris cendré
- **sputtering** = crachotante
- **mantilla** = mantille
- **glittering** = scintillants
- **hem** = ourlet
- **bustled dress** = robe à crinoline

"Old fellows like me can't learn new tricks," he observed profoundly. "It's you youngsters with energy and vitality that have the great future before you."

Far up the road the lights of the Shevlins' country house drifted into view, and presently there was a sighing sound that crept persistently toward them—it might have been the fine plaint of violins or the rustle of the silver wheat under the moon.

They pulled up behind a handsome brougham whose passengers were disembarking at the door. A lady got out, then an elderly gentleman, then another young lady, beautiful as sin. Benjamin started; an almost chemical change seemed to dissolve and recompose the very elements of his body. A rigour passed over him, blood rose into his cheeks, his forehead, and there was a steady thumping in his ears. It was first love.

The girl was slender and frail, with hair that was ashen under the moon and honey-coloured under the sputtering gas-lamps of the porch. Over her shoulders was thrown a Spanish mantilla of softest yellow, butterflied in black; her feet were glittering buttons at the hem of her bustled dress.

Roger Button leaned over to his son. "That," he said, "is young Hildegarde Moncrief, the daughter of General Moncrief."

- **nodded** = acquiesça

- **buggy** = boghei (*petit cabriolet découvert*)

- **reared** = élevé
- **curtsied** = fit une révérence à
- **staggered** = en chancelant

- **dragged out** = s'étira

- **eddied around** = tournoyaient autour de
- **obnoxious** = odieux
- **rosy** = teint rosé
- **whiskers** = favoris

- **his own time** = son tour
- **changing floor** = changement de cavalière
- **drifted out** = se laissèrent emportés
- **melted** = fondirent
- **mantle** = manteau

- **enamel** = des émaux

Benjamin nodded coldly. “Pretty little thing,” he said indifferently. But when the negro boy had led the buggy away, he added: “Dad, you might introduce me to her.”

They approached a group, of which Miss Moncrief was the centre. Reared in the old tradition, she curtsied low before Benjamin. Yes, he might have a dance. He thanked her and walked away—staggered away.

The interval until the time for his turn should arrive dragged itself out interminably. He stood close to the wall, silent, inscrutable, watching with murderous eyes the young bloods of Baltimore as they eddied around Hildegarde Moncrief, passionate admiration in their faces. How obnoxious they seemed to Benjamin; how intolerably rosy! Their curling brown whiskers aroused in him a feeling equivalent to indigestion.

But when his own time came, and he drifted with her out upon the changing floor to the music of the latest waltz from Paris, his jealousies and anxieties melted from him like a mantle of snow. Blind with enchantment, he felt that life was just beginning.

“You and your brother got here just as we did, didn’t you?” asked Hildegarde, looking up at him with eyes that were like bright blue enamel.

- **enlighten her** = la corriger

- **decided against it** = résolut de ne pas le faire
- **mar** = gâcher

- **on the verge of** = sur le point de
- **choked back** = retint

- **worldly-wise** = mondain
- **apt to** = a tendance à

- **mellow** = mûr

- **glorious** = splendide

Benjamin hesitated. If she took him for his father's brother, would it be best to enlighten her? He remembered his experience at Yale, so he decided against it. It would be rude to contradict a lady; it would be criminal to mar this exquisite occasion with the grotesque story of his origin. Later, perhaps. So he nodded, smiled, listened, was happy.

"I like men of your age," Hildegarde told him. "Young boys are so idiotic. They tell me how much champagne they drink at college, and how much money they lose playing cards. Men of your age know how to appreciate women."

Benjamin felt himself on the verge of a proposal—with an effort he choked back the impulse. "You're just the romantic age," she continued—"fifty. Twenty-five is too worldly-wise; thirty is apt to be pale from overwork; forty is the age of long stories that take a whole cigar to tell; sixty is—oh, sixty is too near seventy; but fifty is the mellow age. I love fifty."

Fifty seemed to Benjamin a glorious age. He longed passionately to be fifty.

"I've always said," went on Hildegarde, "that I'd rather marry a man of fifty and be taken care of than marry a man of thirty and take care of *him*."

- **bathed** = baignait
- **mist** = brume

- **in accord on** = s'entendaient sur

- **further** = de manière plus poussée

- **phaeton** = phaéton (*automobile du début du xx*[e] *s.*)
- **crack of dawn** = le point du jour
- **humming** = bourdonnaient
- **glimmered** = se reflétait
- **cool dew** = rosée fraîche
- **wholesale hardware** = quincaillerie en gros

- **nails** = clous

- **absent-mindedly** = distraitement

- **lugs** = écrous (jeu de mots sur la sonorité « *love* » « *lugs* »)

- **dazed** = hébétés
- **an oriole yawned** = un loriot (*petit oiseau jaune et noir*) bâilla
- **piercingly** = de manière perçante
- **quickening** = qui s'animaient

For Benjamin the rest of the evening was bathed in a honey-coloured mist. Hildegarde gave him two more dances, and they discovered that they were marvellously in accord on all the questions of the day. She was to go driving with him on the following Sunday, and then they would discuss all these questions further.

Going home in the phaeton just before the crack of dawn, when the first bees were humming and the fading moon glimmered in the cool dew, Benjamin knew vaguely that his father was discussing wholesale hardware.

".... And what do you think should merit our biggest attention after hammers and nails?" the elder Button was saying.

"Love," replied Benjamin absent-mindedly.

"Lugs?" exclaimed Roger Button, "Why, I've just covered the question of lugs."

Benjamin regarded him with dazed eyes just as the eastern sky was suddenly cracked with light, and an oriole yawned piercingly in the quickening trees...

~

COMPREHENSION

1. Choose the correct words to complete these sentences. (5 pts)

a) At the age of 18, Benjamin Button **tried to/ managed to** enter the university of Yale/Harvard.
b) However, the professors/registrar didn't take him seriously because he looked too **old/young**.
c) Other students **comforted/laughed** at him.

2. Choose the correct answer(s). (10 pts)

A – He started working for his father's company...
a) ...when he was 18.
b) ...when he was 20.
c) ...when he was 22.
d) ...after Yale.

B – Benjamin Button and his father looked...
a) ...like brothers.
b) ...like father and son.
c) ...like cousins.
d) ...very different.

C –The family business is...
a) ...a wholesale hardware company.
b) ...a restaurant.
c) ...in good hands with Benjamin Button.
d) ...thriving.

D – Benjamin Button is...
a) ...reluctant to talk to Hildegarde.
b) ...wants his father to introduce him to Hildegarde.
c) ...not at ease with Hildegarde when they first dance.
d) ...does not think Hildegarde will want to see him again.

E – Hildegarde Moncrief...
a) ...is Roger Button's cousin.
b) ...does not mind Benjamin Button's age.
c) ...does not really like Benjamin Button.
d) ...refuses to marry Benjamin Button.

EXPRESSION

Imagine you are Hildegarde Moncrief and you write a letter to your best friend describing how you met Benjamin Button and how you felt. (5 pts)

Les 10 mots clés

an engagement = les fiançailles
amazingly = de manière spectaculaire
untiringly = infatigablement
atoned = se racheta
to wax stronger = grandir
array = militaire
gaiety = des réjouissances
an ill-matched pair = un couple mal assorti
insidious = insidieuse
a fly in the ointment = une ombre au tableau

Parts VI, VII, and VIII

Benjamin Button's "coming of age" makes him thrive in this world and drives him from marriage to the entertaining life of parties and dance....

~

- **engagement** = fiançailles

- **was made known** = s'était fait connaître
- **sword** = épée

- **feverish pitch** = grande fébrilité

- **John Wilkes Booth** = comédien américain qui assassina le président Lincoln
- **conical horns** = cornes coniques (*attributs associés au diable*)
- **sprouting** = sortaient de

- **played up** = donnèrent du relief

- **solid brass** = bronze massif

- **beau** = galant

VI

When, six months later, the engagement of Miss Hildegarde Moncrief to Mr. Benjamin Button was made known (I say "made known," for General Moncrief declared he would rather fall upon his sword than announce it), the excitement in Baltimore society reached a feverish pitch. The almost forgotten story of Benjamin's birth was remembered and sent out upon the winds of scandal in picaresque and incredible forms. It was said that Benjamin was really the father of Roger Button, that he was his brother who had been in prison for forty years, that he was John Wilkes Booth in disguise—and, finally, that he had two small conical horns sprouting from his head.

The Sunday supplements of the New York papers played up the case with fascinating sketches which showed the head of Benjamin Button attached to a fish, to a snake, and, finally, to a body of solid brass. He became known, journalistically, as the Mystery Man of Maryland. But the true story, as is usually the case, had a very small circulation.

However, every one agreed with General Moncrief that it was "criminal" for a lovely girl who could have married any beau in Baltimore to throw herself into the arms of a man who was assuredly fifty. In vain Mr. Roger Button published his son's birth certificate

- **large type** = gros caractères (d'imprimerie)

- **wavering** = hésitation

- **wholesale hardware business** = quincaillerie de gros
- **mellowness** = maturité

in large type in the Baltimore *Blaze*. No one believed it. You had only to look at Benjamin and see.

On the part of the two people most concerned there was no wavering. So many of the stories about her fiancé were false that Hildegarde refused stubbornly to believe even the true one. In vain General Moncrief pointed out to her the high mortality among men of fifty—or, at least, among men who looked fifty; in vain he told her of the instability of the wholesale hardware business. Hildegarde had chosen to marry for mellowness, and marry she did...

~

- **one particular** = un point particulier

- **amazingly** = de manière spectaculaire

- **retirement** = retraite
- **due largely to** = surtout grâce à

- **needless to say** = inutile de dire que
- **to its bosom** = en son sein
- **son-in-law** = gendre

- **wrought** = avaient opéré
- **flowed** = coulait

- **untiringly** = infatigablement

- **business coup** = coup commercial

- **shipper**= expéditeur
- **statute** = loi

VII

In one particular, at least, the friends of Hildegarde Moncrief were mistaken. The wholesale hardware business prospered amazingly. In the fifteen years between Benjamin Button's marriage in 1880 and his father's retirement in 1895, the family fortune was doubled—and this was due largely to the younger member of the firm.

Needless to say, Baltimore eventually received the couple to its bosom. Even old General Moncrief became reconciled to his son-in-law when Benjamin gave him the money to bring out his *History of the Civil War* in twenty volumes, which had been refused by nine prominent publishers.

In Benjamin himself fifteen years had wrought many changes. It seemed to him that the blood flowed with new vigour through his veins. It began to be a pleasure to rise in the morning, to walk with an active step along the busy, sunny street, to work untiringly with his shipments of hammers and his cargoes of nails. It was in 1890 that he executed his famous business coup: he brought up the suggestion that *all nails used in nailing up the boxes in which nails are shipped are the property of the shippee*, a proposal which became a statute, was approved by Chief Justice Fossile, and saved Roger Button and Company, Wholesale

- **atoned** = se racheta
- **bestowing** = accordant
- **amounted to** = correspondait à

- **it will be well to** = il sera bon de

- **had worshipped her** = l'avait vénérée

- **cheap crockery** = faïence de mauvaise facture
- **placid** = placide
- **anaemic** = anémiée

Hardware, more than *six hundred nails every year.*

In addition, Benjamin discovered that he was becoming more and more attracted by the gay side of life. It was typical of his growing enthusiasm for pleasure that he was the first man in the city of Baltimore to own and run an automobile. Meeting him on the street, his contemporaries would stare enviously at the picture he made of health and vitality.

"He seems to grow younger every year," they would remark. And if old Roger Button, now sixty-five years old, had failed at first to give a proper welcome to his son he atoned at last by bestowing on him what amounted to adulation.

And here we come to an unpleasant subject which it will be well to pass over as quickly as possible. There was only one thing that worried Benjamin Button; his wife had ceased to attract him.

At that time Hildegarde was a woman of thirty-five, with a son, Roscoe, fourteen years old. In the early days of their marriage Benjamin had worshipped her. But, as the years passed, her honey-coloured hair became an unexciting brown, the blue enamel of her eyes assumed the aspect of cheap crockery—moreover, and, most of all, she had become too settled in her ways, too placid, too content, too anaemic in her

- **dragged** = avait traîné
- **were reversed** = étaient inversés

- **inertia** = inertie

- **waxed stronger** = grandissait
- **at the outbreak** = quand éclata

- **charge** = bataille
- **slightly wounded** = légèrement blessé

- **array** = militaire
- **give it up** = y renoncer
- **required attention** = demandait de l'attention
- **brass band** = fanfare

excitements, and too sober in her taste. As a bride it had been she who had "dragged" Benjamin to dances and dinners—now conditions were reversed. She went out socially with him, but without enthusiasm, devoured already by that eternal inertia which comes to live with each of us one day and stays with us to the end.

Benjamin's discontent waxed stronger. At the outbreak of the Spanish-American War in 1898 his home had for him so little charm that he decided to join the army. With his business influence he obtained a commission as captain, and proved so adaptable to the work that he was made a major, and finally a lieutenant-colonel just in time to participate in the celebrated charge up San Juan Hill. He was slightly wounded, and received a medal.

Benjamin had become so attached to the activity and excitement of array life that he regretted to give it up, but his business required attention, so he resigned his commission and came home. He was met at the station by a brass band and escorted to his house.

- **waving** = en agitant
- **silk flag** = drapeau de soie
- **sinking of the heart** = pincement au cœur
- **had taken their toll** = avaient eu un effet néfaste
- **skirmish** = en bataille

- **delighted** = ravi
- **uneasy** = embarrassé
- **hitherto** = jusque-là
- **bodily** = physique

- **shuddered** = tressaillit

- **annoyed** = contrariée

- **amiss** = qui n’allait pas
- **relieve** = soulager

VIII

Hildegarde, waving a large silk flag, greeted him on the porch, and even as he kissed her he felt with a sinking of the heart that these three years had taken their toll. She was a woman of forty now, with a faint skirmish line of gray hairs in her head. The sight depressed him.

Up in his room he saw his reflection in the familiar mirror—he went closer and examined his own face with anxiety, comparing it after a moment with a photograph of himself in uniform taken just before the war.

"Good Lord!" he said aloud. The process was continuing. There was no doubt of it—he looked now like a man of thirty. Instead of being delighted, he was uneasy—he was growing younger. He had hitherto hoped that once he reached a bodily age equivalent to his age in years, the grotesque phenomenon which had marked his birth would cease to function. He shuddered. His destiny seemed to him awful, incredible.

When he came downstairs Hildegarde was waiting for him. She appeared annoyed, and he wondered if she had at last discovered that there was something amiss. It was with an effort to relieve the tension between

- **broached the matter** = aborda le sujet

- **scorn** = mépris
- **sniffed** = fit la moue
- **boast about** = se vanter
- **asserted** = affirma

- **should think** = j'aurais pensé

- **retorted** = répliqua

- **made up your mind** = as décidé d'être

- **considerate** = délicat

- **I can't help it** = je n'y peux rien

- **You can too.** = Bien sûr que si.
- **stubborn** = entêté

them that he broached the matter at dinner in what he considered a delicate way.

"Well," he remarked lightly, "everybody says I look younger than ever."

Hildegarde regarded him with scorn. She sniffed. "Do you think it's anything to boast about?"

"I'm not boasting," he asserted uncomfortably. She sniffed again. "The idea," she said, and after a moment: "I should think you'd have enough pride to stop it."

"How can I?" he demanded.

"I'm not going to argue with you," she retorted. "But there's a right way of doing things and a wrong way. If you've made up your mind to be different from everybody else, I don't suppose I can stop you, but I really don't think it's very considerate."

"But, Hildegarde, I can't help it."

"You can too. You're simply stubborn. You think you don't want to be like any one else. You always have been that way, and you always will be. But just think how it would be if every one else looked at things as you do—what would the world be like?"

- **inane** = inepte

- **chasm** = abîme

- **breach** = rupture
- **gathered headway** = prenait son essor
- **gaiety** = réjouissances

- **chatting** = discutant
- **dowager** = douairière
- **evil omen** = mauvais augure
- **chaperons** = chaperons (*accompagnateurs des jeunes filles*)
- **haughty disapproval** = réprobation hautaine
- **puzzled** = perplexes

- **What a pity!** = Quelle tristesse !
- **fellow** = garçon

- **ill-matched pair** = couple mal assorti

- **took up** = se mit au
- **the Boston** = le boston (*danse de l'époque*)
- **proficient** = compétent
- **Maxine** = la matchiche (*danse de l'époque*)

As this was an inane and unanswerable argument Benjamin made no reply, and from that time on a chasm began to widen between them. He wondered what possible fascination she had ever exercised over him.

To add to the breach, he found, as the new century gathered headway, that his thirst for gaiety grew stronger. Never a party of any kind in the city of Baltimore but he was there, dancing with the prettiest of the young married women, chatting with the most popular of the débutantes, and finding their company charming, while his wife, a dowager of evil omen, sat among the chaperons, now in haughty disapproval, and now following him with solemn, puzzled, and reproachful eyes.

"Look!" people would remark. "What a pity! A young fellow that age tied to a woman of forty-five. He must be twenty years younger than his wife." They had forgotten—as people inevitably forget—that back in 1880 their mammas and papas had also remarked about this same ill-matched pair.

Benjamin's growing unhappiness at home was compensated for by his many new interests. He took up golf and made a great success of it. He went in for dancing: in 1906 he was an expert at "The Boston," and in 1908 he was considered proficient at the "Maxine,"

- **Castle Walk** = le castle walk (*danse de l'époque*)

- **to some extent** = dans un certaine mesure

- **hand it on to** = confier à

- **mistaken for each other** = confondus
- **pleased** = plaisait à
- **insidious** = insidieuse

- **there was one fly in the delicious ointment** = il y avait juste une ombre au beau tableau
- **the sight of her** = sa vue

while in 1909 his "Castle Walk" was the envy of every young man in town.

His social activities, of course, interfered to some extent with his business, but then he had worked hard at wholesale hardware for twenty-five years and felt that he could soon hand it on to his son, Roscoe, who had recently graduated from Harvard.

He and his son were, in fact, often mistaken for each other. This pleased Benjamin—he soon forgot the insidious fear which had come over him on his return from the Spanish-American War, and grew to take a naïve pleasure in his appearance. There was only one fly in the delicious ointment—he hated to appear in public with his wife. Hildegarde was almost fifty, and the sight of her made him feel absurd....

COMPREHENSION

1. True or false? (4 pts)

a) Hildegarde Moncrief and Benjamin Button looked the same age.
b) Benjamin was not really busy.
c) Benjamin refused to join the army.
d) Hildegarde started to criticized Benjamin because he looked younger and younger.

2. Choose the correct answer to complete the sentences. (4 pts)

A – Benjamin Button looked .... when Hidegarde decided to marry him.

a) fifty
b) thirty

B – Benjamin was the first man to own .... in Baltimore

a) a motorbike
b) an automobile

C – At the end of the Spanish-American War, Benjamin Button was welcome with ....

a) laughter and mockery.
b) a brass band.

D – When Hildegarde was about fifty, he started to feel...

a) ashamed of being with her.
b) increasingly happy at home.

3. What do the following expressions mean exactly? Choose the correct answer. (4 pts)

A – "The mystery man of Maryland":
- a) Roger Button
- b) Benjamin Button

B – The "outbreak of the Spanish-American War":
- a) the beginning of the war
- b) the end of the war

C – "Array life":
- a) leisure
- b) military life

D – Benjamin's "thirst for gaiety":
- a) his interest in books
- b) his interest in parties and dance

EXPRESSION

1. Benjamin Button's father and Hildegarde engage in a conversation about Benjamin. Imagine the discussion. (4 pts)
2. Imagine you are Benjamin Button and you write his diary describing the evolution of his life with Hildegarde. (4 pts)

Les 10 mots clés

a freshman = un étudiant de première année
a sophomore = un étudiant de deuxième année
to play soldier = jouer aux soldats
weeping = en pleurs
childish = enfantin
a grubby boy = un petit enfant crasseux
mats and chains = des colliers
kindergarten = le jardin d'enfants
to fade = s'effacer
to enlist = s'engager

Parts IX, X, and XI

Becoming a man, becoming a father while going from university to kindergarten... Benjamin grows old but looks younger and younger... How can a baby have lived such a wonderful life? Why does "the warm sweet aroma of the milk" take on a new meaning, filled with the emotion of both a new-born child and a dying old man...?

~

- **handded over to** = avait été cédé à

- **entered himself** = s'inscrivit
- **freshman** = étudiant de première année

- **had been graduated** = avait reçu un diplôme

- **prominent** = de choix

- **dash** = panache
- **touchdowns** = essais
- **one entire eleven** = une équipe entière
- **singly** = un à un
- **college** = l'université

- **junior year** = troisième année universitaire
- **scarcely** = à peine
- **"make"**= rejoindre

IX

One September day in 1910—a few years after Roger Button & Co., Wholesale Hardware, had been handed over to young Roscoe Button—a man, apparently about twenty years old, entered himself as a freshman at Harvard University in Cambridge. He did not make the mistake of announcing that he would never see fifty again, nor did he mention the fact that his son had been graduated from the same institution ten years before.

He was admitted, and almost immediately attained a prominent position in the class, partly because he seemed a little older than the other freshmen, whose average age was about eighteen.

But his success was largely due to the fact that in the football game with Yale he played so brilliantly, with so much dash and with such a cold, remorseless anger that he scored seven touchdowns and fourteen field goals for Harvard, and caused one entire eleven of Yale men to be carried singly from the field, unconscious. He was the most celebrated man in college.

Strange to say, in his third or junior year he was scarcely able to "make" the team. The coaches said that he had lost weight, and it seemed to the more observant among them that he was not quite as tall

- **chiefly** = principalement

- **slight** = mince
- **frail** = frêle
- **sophomores** = étudiant de deuxième année
- **something of** = quelque chose de l'ordre du

- **worldliness** = matérialisme
-
- **advanced** = avancées
- **preparatory school** = école qui prépare à l'université

- **sheltered life** = l'environnement protecteur
- **congenial** = profitable

- **obviously** = de toute évidence
- **heartiness** = cordialité

- **moped** = traînait
- **mooniness** = rêvasserie

as before. He made no touchdowns—indeed, he was retained on the team chiefly in hope that his enormous reputation would bring terror and disorganisation to the Yale team.

In his senior year he did not make the team at all. He had grown so slight and frail that one day he was taken by some sophomores for a freshman, an incident which humiliated him terribly. He became known as something of a prodigy—a senior who was surely no more than sixteen—and he was often shocked at the worldliness of some of his classmates. His studies seemed harder to him—he felt that they were too advanced. He had heard his classmates speak of St. Midas's, the famous preparatory school, at which so many of them had prepared for college, and he determined after his graduation to enter himself at St. Midas's, where the sheltered life among boys his own size would be more congenial to him.

Upon his graduation in 1914 he went home to Baltimore with his Harvard diploma in his pocket. Hildegarde was now residing in Italy, so Benjamin went to live with his son, Roscoe. But though he was welcomed in a general way there was obviously no heartiness in Roscoe's feeling toward him—there was even perceptible a tendency on his son's part to think that Benjamin, as he moped about the house in adolescent mooniness, was somewhat in the way. Roscoe was

- **creep out** = se révèle

- **college set** = étudiants

- **recurred to him** = lui revint

- **distasteful** = désagréable

- **helplessly** = impuissant

- **narrowed** = plissa les yeux
- **uneasily** = mal à l'aise
- **pull up short** = t'arrêter immédiatement

- **crimsoned** = s'empourpra
- **sought for** = cherchait

- **behave yourself** = tiens-toi bien

married now and prominent in Baltimore life, and he wanted no scandal to creep out in connection with his family.

Benjamin, no longer *persona grata* with the débutantes and younger college set, found himself left much alone, except for the companionship of three or four fifteen-year-old boys in the neighbourhood. His idea of going to St. Midas's school recurred to him.

"Say," he said to Roscoe one day, "I've told you over and over that I want to go to prep school."

"Well, go, then," replied Roscoe shortly. The matter was distasteful to him, and he wished to avoid a discussion.

"I can't go alone," said Benjamin helplessly. "You'll have to enter me and take me up there."

"I haven't got time," declared Roscoe abruptly. His eyes narrowed and he looked uneasily at his father. "As a matter of fact," he added, "you'd better not go on with this business much longer. You better pull up short. You better—you better"—he paused and his face crimsoned as he sought for words—"you better turn right around and start back the other way. This has gone too far to be a joke. It isn't funny any longer. You—you behave yourself!"

- **on the verge of tears** = au bord des larmes

- **harsh** = sévère

Benjamin looked at him, on the verge of tears.

"And another thing," continued Roscoe, "when visitors are in the house I want you to call me 'Uncle'—not 'Roscoe,' but 'Uncle,' do you understand? It looks absurd for a boy of fifteen to call me by my first name. Perhaps you'd better call me 'Uncle' *all* the time, so you'll get used to it."

With a harsh look at his father, Roscoe turned away...

~

- **dismally** = de manière nonchalante

- **faint** = léger
- **down** = duvet
- **meddle** = toucher

- **imitation whiskers** = postiche
- **cheeks** = joues
- **farce** = mascarade
- **itched** = le démangeait
- **made him ashamed** = lui faisait honte
- **had reluctantly relented** = avait cédé à contre-cœur

- **persistently** = avec obstination

- **enlist** = s'engager (dans l'armée)
- **alas** = hélas

- **butler** = majordome
- **legend** = légende
- **tore it open eagerly** = la déchira pour l'ouvrir en toute hâte
- **enclosure** = contenu
- **reserve officers** = officiers de réserve

X

At the termination of this interview, Benjamin wandered dismally upstairs and stared at himself in the mirror. He had not shaved for three months, but he could find nothing on his face but a faint white down with which it seemed unnecessary to meddle. When he had first come home from Harvard, Roscoe had approached him with the proposition that he should wear eye-glasses and imitation whiskers glued to his cheeks, and it had seemed for a moment that the farce of his early years was to be repeated. But whiskers had itched and made him ashamed. He wept and Roscoe had reluctantly relented.

Benjamin opened a book of boys' stories, *The Boy Scouts in Bimini Bay*, and began to read. But he found himself thinking persistently about the war. America had joined the Allied cause during the preceding month, and Benjamin wanted to enlist, but, alas, sixteen was the minimum age, and he did not look that old. His true age, which was fifty-seven, would have disqualified him, anyway.

There was a knock at his door, and the butler appeared with a letter bearing a large official legend in the corner and addressed to Mr. Benjamin Button. Benjamin tore it open eagerly, and read the enclosure with delight. It informed him that many reserve officers who had

- **commission** = nomination
- **report** = rejoindre son unité

- **fairly quivering** = plutôt frémissant

- **seized** = prit

- **treble** = aiguë

- **play soldier** = jouer au soldat
- **clerk** = commis
- **casually** = avec désinvolture
- **flushed** = rougit

- **I'm good for it** = je tiens la route

- **the proper** = appropriés pour
- **dealer** = tailleur
- **Y.W.C.A.** = Young Women Christian Association

served in the Spanish-American War were being called back into service with a higher rank, and it enclosed his commission as brigadier-general in the United States army with orders to report immediately.

Benjamin jumped to his feet fairly quivering with enthusiasm. This was what he had wanted. He seized his cap, and ten minutes later he had entered a large tailoring establishment on Charles Street, and asked in his uncertain treble to be measured for a uniform.

"Want to play soldier, sonny?" demanded a clerk casually.

Benjamin flushed. "Say! Never mind what I want!" he retorted angrily. "My name's Button and I live on Mt. Vernon Place, so you know I'm good for it."

"Well," admitted the clerk hesitantly, "if you're not, I guess your daddy is, all right."

Benjamin was measured, and a week later his uniform was completed. He had difficulty in obtaining the proper general's insignia because the dealer kept insisting to Benjamin that a nice Y.W.C.A. badge would look just as well and be much more fun to play with.

Saying nothing to Roscoe, he left the house one night

- **sultry** = suffocant

- **sentry** = sentinelle

- **handle** = s'occuper de
- **briskly** = d'un ton brusque

- **eyed him reproachfully** = lui jeta un regard réprobateur
- **duds** = fringues

- **whirled** = fusilla du regard
- **treble voice** = voix aiguë

- **thunder** = tonner

- **snap his heels** = claquer ses talons

- **obedience** = obéissance

- **shrilly** = d'une voix stridente

- **drew rein** = tira sur sa bride
- **twinkle** = pétillement (malicieux)
- **kindly** = gentiment

and proceeded by train to Camp Mosby, in South Carolina, where he was to command an infantry brigade. On a sultry April day he approached the entrance to the camp, paid off the taxicab which had brought him from the station, and turned to the sentry on guard.

"Get some one to handle my luggage!" he said briskly.

The sentry eyed him reproachfully. "Say," he remarked, "where you goin' with the general's duds, sonny?"

Benjamin, veteran of the Spanish-American War, whirled upon him with fire in his eye, but with, alas, a changing treble voice.

"Come to attention!" he tried to thunder; he paused for breath—then suddenly he saw the sentry snap his heels together and bring his rifle to the present. Benjamin concealed a smile of gratification, but when he glanced around his smile faded. It was not he who had inspired obedience, but an imposing artillery colonel who was approaching on horseback.

"Colonel!" called Benjamin shrilly.

The colonel came up, drew rein, and looked coolly down at him with a twinkle in his eyes. "Whose little boy are you?" he demanded kindly.

- **darn well** = un peu

- **roared** = rugit

- **Here!** = Tenez !
- **thrust** = tendit brutalement

- **his eyes popping from their sockets** = avec les yeux exorbités

- **headquarters** = quartier général
- **talk this over** = discuter de tout ça

- **meanwhile** = tout en
- **stern** = âpre

"I'll soon darn well show you whose little boy I am!" retorted Benjamin in a ferocious voice. "Get down off that horse!"

The colonel roared with laughter.

"You want him, eh, general?"

"Here!" cried Benjamin desperately. "Read this." And he thrust his commission toward the colonel.

The colonel read it, his eyes popping from their sockets.

"Where'd you get this?" he demanded, slipping the document into his own pocket.

"I got it from the Government, as you'll soon find out!"

"You come along with me," said the colonel with a peculiar look. "We'll go up to headquarters and talk this over. Come along."

The colonel turned and began walking his horse in the direction of headquarters. There was nothing for Benjamin to do but follow with as much dignity as possible—meanwhile promising himself a stern revenge.

- **materialise** = se concrétiser

- **hot and cross** = échauffé et courroucé
- **hasty** = précipité
- **weeping** = en pleurs

But this revenge did not materialise. Two days later, however, his son Roscoe materialised from Baltimore, hot and cross from a hasty trip, and escorted the weeping general, *sans* uniform, back to his home.

~

- **attendant** = qui s'ensuivirent
- **thought it "the thing"** = ne pensèrent pas nécessaire
- **grubby boy** = petit garçon crasseux

- **a hint of** = un soupçon de
- **torment** = tourment
- **idiom** = la langue

- **red-blooded he-man** = homme avec de la trempe

- **to the edge of insanity** = à la limite de la folie
- **live wires** = gens montés sur des ressorts
- **on such a scale** = à cette échelle-là

- **childish** = d'enfant

- **kindergarten** = jardin d'enfants
- **strips of paper** = bandes de papier
- **mats and chains** = des colliers

XI

In 1920 Roscoe Button's first child was born. During the attendant festivities, however, no one thought it "the thing" to mention, that the little grubby boy, apparently about ten years of age who played around the house with lead soldiers and a miniature circus, was the new baby's own grandfather.

No one disliked the little boy whose fresh, cheerful face was crossed with just a hint of sadness, but to Roscoe Button his presence was a source of torment. In the idiom of his generation Roscoe did not consider the matter "efficient." It seemed to him that his father, in refusing to look sixty, had not behaved like a "red-blooded he-man"—this was Roscoe's favourite expression—but in a curious and perverse manner. Indeed, to think about the matter for as much as a half an hour drove him to the edge of insanity. Roscoe believed that "live wires" should keep young, but carrying it out on such a scale was—was—was inefficient. And there Roscoe rested.

Five years later Roscoe's little boy had grown old enough to play childish games with little Benjamin under the supervision of the same nurse. Roscoe took them both to kindergarten on the same day, and Benjamin found that playing with little strips of coloured paper, making mats and chains and curious

- **was bad** = s'était mal comporté

- **tousled hair** = les cheveux ébouriffés

- **tots** = bambins

- **dim** = de manière obscure

- **he was never to** = il ne pourrait jamais

- **flowed on** = s'écoulaient
- **went back** = retourna

- **starched gingham dress** = robe vichy amidonnée

and beautiful designs, was the most fascinating game in the world. Once he was bad and had to stand in the corner—then he cried—but for the most part there were gay hours in the cheerful room, with the sunlight coming in the windows and Miss Bailey's kind hand resting for a moment now and then in his tousled hair.

Roscoe's son moved up into the first grade after a year, but Benjamin stayed on in the kindergarten. He was very happy. Sometimes when other tots talked about what they would do when they grew up a shadow would cross his little face as if in a dim, childish way he realised that those were things in which he was never to share.

The days flowed on in monotonous content. He went back a third year to the kindergarten, but he was too little now to understand what the bright shining strips of paper were for. He cried because the other boys were bigger than he, and he was afraid of them. The teacher talked to him, but though he tried to understand he could not understand at all.

He was taken from the kindergarten. His nurse, Nana, in her starched gingham dress, became the centre of his tiny world. On bright days they walked in the park; Nana would point at a great gray monster and say "elephant," and Benjamin would say it after her, and when he was being undressed for bed that night

- **bounce you up** = rebondir

- **hat-rack** = portemanteau

- **cluck at** = regardaient en gloussant

- **submitted to** = se plia
- **boredom** = lassitude
- **oatmeal** = porridge
- **mushy** = bouillies

- **troublesome** = dérangeantes
- **token** = souvenir
- **flustered** = faisait palpiter

- **crib** = berceau

- **twilight** = crépuscule

- **haunt** = hanter

- **at the head of his men** = à la tête de sa troupe

he would say it over and over aloud to her: "Elyphant, elyphant, elyphant." Sometimes Nana let him jump on the bed, which was fun, because if you sat down exactly right it would bounce you up on your feet again, and if you said "Ah" for a long time while you jumped you got a very pleasing broken vocal effect.

He loved to take a big cane from the hat-rack and go around hitting chairs and tables with it and saying: "Fight, fight, fight." When there were people there the old ladies would cluck at him, which interested him, and the young ladies would try to kiss him, which he submitted to with mild boredom. And when the long day was done at five o'clock he would go upstairs with Nana and be fed on oatmeal and nice soft mushy foods with a spoon.

There were no troublesome memories in his childish sleep; no token came to him of his brave days at college, of the glittering years when he flustered the hearts of many girls. There were only the white, safe walls of his crib and Nana and a man who came to see him sometimes, and a great big orange ball that Nana pointed at just before his twilight bed hour and called "sun." When the sun went his eyes were sleepy—there were no dreams, no dreams to haunt him.

The past—the wild charge at the head of his men up San Juan Hill; the first years of his marriage when he

- **dusk** = tombée de la nuit

- **gloomy** = lugubre
- **had faded** = s'étaient effacés
- **unsubstantial** = immatériels

- **noons** = jours
- **mumblings** = marmonnements
- **scarcely** = à peine
- **faintly** = à peine

- **crib** = berceau
- **dim** = indistincts
- **faded out** = s'effacèrent

worked late into the summer dusk down in the busy city for young Hildegarde whom he loved; the days before that when he sat smoking far into the night in the gloomy old Button house on Monroe Street with his grandfather-all these had faded like unsubstantial dreams from his mind as though they had never been. He did not remember.

He did not remember clearly whether the milk was warm or cool at his last feeding or how the days passed—there was only his crib and Nana's familiar presence. And then he remembered nothing. When he was hungry he cried—that was all. Through the noons and nights he breathed and over him there were soft mumblings and murmurings that he scarcely heard, and faintly differentiated smells, and light and darkness.

Then it was all dark, and his white crib and the dim faces that moved above him, and the warm sweet aroma of the milk, faded out altogether from his mind.

~

COMPREHENSION

1. Quiz (6 pts)

A – Who enters Harvard University in 1910?

a) Roscoe
b) Benjamin
c) Roger
d) Hildegarde

B – In his third year at university, how were his physical capacities?

a) He was taller and better at football.
b) He was smaller and could hardly enter the football team.
c) He remained the best at football.
d) He scored even more touchdowns than before.

C – Why doesn't Roscoe want his father to call him "Roscoe"?

a) Because he has become a real man and wants to be called Mr Button.
b) Because Benjamin looks fifteen and should call Roscoe "Uncle."
c) Because they both look similar and they should be thought of as brothers.
d) Because he has another nickname.

2 – Fill in the blanks with the appropriate words. (4 pts)

dark / grandson / memory / nurse /
reduced / speak / words / world

In the final chapter, Benjamin becomes younger and younger and can play with his ________. He has a ________, called Nana, who looks after him. As time goes by, Benjamin knows fewer and fewer ________ and ends up not being able to ________. His ________ starts to fail him and the ___________around him becomes more and more blurred and __________. Eventually, it becomes ________.

EXPRESSION

1. What are the moments that you found most moving in this story? (2 pts)
2. What are the moments that made you smile? (2 pts)
3. If this story were told in today's world, would something have to change in the plot? (2 pts)
4. Write your own review of the story, explaining why you liked or disliked it, what struck you the most. (2 pts)
5. Write the pitch of the story to make people read this story. (2 pts)

Achevé d'imprimer sur les presses
d'Evoluprint en France, octobre 2022